What Did I Do to Deserve a Sister Like You?

What Did I Do to Deserve a Sister Like You?

Angela Shelf Medearis
Illustrated by Robert Papp

AN
APPLE
PAPERBACK

SCHOLASTIC INC.

New York   Toronto   London   Auckland   Sydney
Mexico City   New Delhi   Hong Kong   Buenos Aires

12 11   6 7 8/0
                                                                                40

Printed in the U.S.A.
First Scholastic printing, February 2003

*To my friend and big sister Sandra Fergins,
and to my friend and "pretend" sister Brigid Cockrum
and her family, with love and thanks.
What did I do to deserve such
wonderful people in my life like you?
Love always, Angela*

Contents

Chapter One

~~~~~~

Introducing Sharie and Sandra

I hate Thursdays, even though today is the next to the last day of school. Thursday is the day my big sister Sandra and I have to go to piano lessons at Mrs. Harmon's house. I'd rather eat liver and onions for breakfast than go to piano lessons.

Sandra always takes forever to get ready and won't let me in the bathroom. She was in there for at least an hour today, combing and recombing her hair.

"Sandra," I yelled. "Quit staring at yourself in the mirror before you break it!"

"Shut up, Sharie," Sandra said through the door. "I'll bet when you look in the mirror you disappear, just like all the rest of the vampires."

1

I kicked the door but I was too mad to say anything. Sandra is always saying things that make me feel bad about myself. The sad thing is that most of the time she's telling the truth.

I must admit that Sandra got all the looks in the family. She has beautiful creamy brown skin, coal black curly hair, big brown eyes, and long eyelashes. I don't know what happened to me. My hair looks like it's plugged into a 200-volt live wire. My eyes are hidden by thick, ugly glasses. I have to wear them because I'm very nearsighted. Worst of all, here it is almost the last day of school, and I'm already getting the horrible eczema rash I get every summer. Momma says it runs in the family, but I'm the only one I know who has it. I think I'm allergic to Sandra.

I would love to be beautiful, but I guess life's like that. Momma says I'm just a late bloomer. She says all girls go through a stage where they look like I do. I don't think so. I've seen pictures of Sandra when she was ten, and she looks pretty. As far as I can tell, Sandra has been pretty all of her life. She looks just like Momma. I don't know who I look like. Sometimes I feel like I'm an alien and I was left on my family's doorstep!

It wouldn't be so bad if Sandra was good-looking and that was it. She does almost everything she tries perfectly, too. She's captain of the cheerleading squad, class president, and she can play six different musical instruments. My only talent is my ability to cross my eyes and touch my tongue to my nose.

"Okay, Vampira," Sandra said as she opened the bathroom door. "I'm ready."

She misted herself with perfume and smiled at her reflection one last time.

I started to cough. "People are going to be able to smell you before they even see you."

"Well, at least I don't smell like a pile of gym socks," Sandra said.

"How do you know? You use so much of that stuff I'll bet your nasal passages are all clogged up. This is what you really smell like." I made a long, low raspberry.

"You're about as funny as you look," Sandra said. "Aren't you going to comb your hair?"

I glanced at myself in the mirror. My hair was sticking up all over. I raked my fingers through it. It looked okay to me.

"Now, let's go," I said. "If we hurry, we'll be home in time for *Spooky Theater*."

"Big deal," Sandra said. "I don't know why you watch that dumb program. It always scares you so bad you can't go to sleep at night."

"You should watch it, too," I said. "All the creatures from outer space look just like you."

Sandra tried to hit me but I was too fast for her. She chased me all the way to Mrs. Harmon's house. Too bad we were running *to* our piano lessons instead of running *away* from them.

The main reason I hate going to piano lessons is that if I play a wrong note, Mrs. Harmon slaps my hands. Think about it, I spend more time getting my hands slapped than I do playing. I know it would help if I practiced, but I hate it! According to Mrs. Harmon, I am one of the worst piano players in the world. After three years, I'm still working on the beginner book called "Sweet, Simple Songs." None of

5

the songs seem that simple to me. I still can't play any of them all the way through.

I haven't told anyone, not even my best friend Annette, but I have a big secret. I'm afraid of playing in Mrs. Harmon's piano recital more than anything else in the whole world. I know that as soon as I try to play my song, everyone — even Momma — will laugh at me. I sound horrible! I decided there was no way I was going to play in that recital and make a fool out of myself. I had to think up a way to get out of it, or I was going to be in *big* trouble.

Chapter Two

Trouble at Mrs. Harmon's House

"How's my star pupil?" Mrs. Harmon asked with a smile when she saw my sister. "Ready to play that grand finale tomorrow?"

"Yes, I've been practicing real hard," Sandra said.

"Good, good," Mrs. Harmon said. "I know I can count on you."

I pushed Sandra out of the way and walked in the front door.

"Hi, Mrs. Harmon," I said.

Mrs. Harmon's whole face changed when she saw me. She frowned and rolled her eyes up to the sky. "Hello, Sharie," she mumbled. "How are you coming along with your recital song?"

"Oh, I've got the first three notes down," I said. "But the rest of the first line is giving me a lot of trouble."

"Have you been practicing?" Mrs. Harmon asked.

"No," Sandra said quickly.

"*Yes*," I said. "She's not talking to you Sandra, so mind your own business."

"She hasn't touched the piano all week," Sandra tattled.

"How can I, when you've been on it most of the time?"

"Now, now," Mrs. Harmon said. "That's enough. Let's get started. Come on, Sandra. Let's hear your lesson first."

I went into the den and flopped down on the couch. I looked around for something to read until it was my turn to play. I bet Mrs. Harmon hasn't thrown anything away since she was born. There's so much dust on her furniture that sometimes I write on it while I'm waiting for my lesson. Whatever I've written is usually there when I come back. A long time ago I wrote "HELP, HELP, PLEASE DUST ME!" on the end table. Sure enough, it was still there today.

The love of Mrs. Harmon's life is her old bulldog, Mickey. He sleeps underneath the piano most of the time. At first, I thought Mickey was a stuffed dog because he didn't move. Then he drooled on my shoe while I was pressing on one of the foot pedals. Gross! He's definitely alive.

Mrs. Harmon and Mickey look a lot alike. Mickey is really fat and wheezes when he walks, which is not too often. Come to think of it, so does Mrs. Harmon. Mrs. Harmon wears dentures that don't fit very well, so she sprays a lot of spit whenever she talks. Mickey drools all the time, too. They're both real old, have wrinkly brown faces, and the same mean expression in their eyes. I've heard of people looking like their pets, but Mrs. Harmon and Mickey look almost like twins.

"Okay, Sharie," Mrs. Harmon called from the other room with a sigh. "It's your turn."

I got my music out of my backpack. I felt like I was

going in front of a firing squad. "I brought earplugs," Sandra whispered as she passed by me.

"Stick them up your nose," I whispered back.

"What did you say?" Mrs. Harmon asked.

"I said you smell like a rose."

"Thank you, Sharie. That's very sweet," Mrs. Harmon said. A shower of spittle flew across the room. I ducked out of the way. "Now, let's hear you play your recital song."

I started to play "The Babbling Brook" for Mrs. Harmon. I hit a whole bunch of wrong notes when I was playing the babbling part of the song. Mrs. Harmon cracked my hand a good one. Boy, did it hurt! First Sandra made me mad and now her. I jumped off the piano stool and just exploded.

"Ouch! That hurt!" I yelled. "Why are you so mean?"

Mrs. Harmon was furious! "Young lady," she said, tugging on her red wig and spraying spit everywhere, "you are the rudest child I have ever taught! I don't know how you think you're going to play in my special recital tomorrow evening!"

"Well, I just won't play!" I shouted. "I HATE PI-ANO LESSONS!"

Mrs. Harmon worked her dentures back into place and glared at me. Old Mickey woke up with a snort and glared at me, too. Then he started growling and barking. I thought Mrs. Harmon was going to sic Mickey on me, but I guess he's too fat for that kind of stuff. Mickey probably wears dentures, too. Sandra heard all the yelling and barking and came running into the room.

"Sharie Johnson," Sandra said, "you're in big trouble now! I'm going to tell Momma on you!"

I suddenly felt sick. If Momma knew I'd yelled at Mrs. Harmon, I'd be grounded all summer! I'd never get to ride the roller coaster at Joyland Amusement Park! What was I going to do?

Chapter Three

The Bargain

I was afraid Sandra would tell Momma that I'd lost my temper, but I wasn't going to let her know it. I picked up my music and got ready to leave.

"Sandra, I'm *not* going to apologize because I'm *not* sorry. You just mind your own business."

"I'm going to tell my mother about this right away, Mrs. Harmon," Sandra said. "I'm real sorry about Sharie's behavior."

"It's not your fault, child," said Mrs. Harmon as she patted Sandra on the shoulder. I guess she was giving Sandra a pretty good spit shower, because Sandra backed away from her real quick. Sandra frowned and rubbed her arm across her face.

"Good-bye, Mrs. Harmon," Sandra said. "I'll see you at the recital tomorrow evening." I rushed out of that old musty room as fast as I could. I was going to try to beat Sandra home. I knew exactly what I was going to do. I'd call Momma at work and tell her my side of the story. Momma always says honesty is the best policy. Besides, I'd tell her about Mrs. Harmon almost breaking my fingers. Maybe she'd understand why I was so mad. Maybe Momma would say that I didn't have to play in the recital! That would solve all my problems.

I took off down the street. I could still hear Mickey barking as I ran down the block. Then I heard something else — footsteps! Sandra was trying to outrun me! She was going to call Momma before I did!

I had a pretty good head start, but Sandra caught up with me in no time. She can really move on those long legs of hers when she wants to.

"Sharie, you know Momma said we're supposed to walk home together," she said as she grabbed my arm.

Sandra started working me over about what she was going to tell Momma. She said she was going to make sure I had to wash dishes for the rest of my life for yelling at Mrs. Harmon. Sandra knows how much I want to go to Joyland Amusement Park, so she said the only way I'd get to see it was if I was passing by the sign on the street. But I have to go to Joyland! This is the first year I can ride on the roller coaster by myself!

I pretended like I didn't care, but I was starting to get scared. Momma doesn't like us to be sassy to older people. She'd ground me for the rest of the summer if she found out what I said to Mrs. Harmon.

We were passing by McGregor's Grocery when Robert Nickols came out of the store. He's one of the cutest boys at Sandra's school. She is crazy about him. Sometimes I think that Sandra has lost her mind over that boy. She took her yearbook to the copy store and blew up Robert's class pictures. Then she pasted them all over her room. They have a class together, and if Robert so much as breathes in her direction Sandra walks around bumping into walls. When Sandra saw Robert, I thought her teeth were going to fall out. If it hadn't been for her braces, they probably would have.

I've wondered if Sandra has been sneaking around to see Robert, but I never have caught her. Momma doesn't allow Sandra to date yet. She wants Sandra to concentrate on her grades and her music. Momma is very strict about that. If she knew Sandra was seeing Robert, she would be in big trouble.

It must have been my lucky day! The first thing Robert said to Sandra was, "Why didn't you call me last night?"

"Oooh," I said, "you just wait till I tell Momma you've been dating, Sandra!"

Sandra pinched my arm so hard I yelled. She smiled at Robert until the sunlight bounced off her braces. "I'm in a big hurry right now, Robert," Sandra said. "I'll talk to you later."

"I bet you will," I said. Sandra grabbed my arm again and jerked me down the street. I yanked my arm away from her.

"Momma's going to ground you when she finds out you've been talking to Robert," I said.

I couldn't wait to run home and tell Momma on *her* for a change. Sandra looked guilty. She rubbed her forehead and licked her lips nervously. For the first time, I, Sharie Johnson, Super Detective, finally had evidence on Miss Perfect. *Yes!*

"Look, Sharie," said Sandra, smiling slyly. "I'll make a deal with you. If you promise not to tell on me, I won't tell Momma about Mrs. Harmon. I'll even let you go with me the next time I go to Joyland. Okay?"

Oh, brother, I'd forgotten all about old Mrs. Harmon. I felt like I had been robbed. Man, the only time in history I had something on Sandra, and I couldn't even use it!

"Okay," I said finally. For a minute, I felt good. All my problems were solved. Then I remembered the piano recital. I had to think of a way to get out of playing in that recital, but what could I do?

Chapter Four

The Best-Laid Plans

When Sandra and I got home from piano lessons, I flopped down on the couch. I tried to watch *Spooky Theater,* but I couldn't concentrate. The thought of trying to play the piano in front of hundreds of people was scarier than anything they had on television. I started to think of all the ways I could get out of it.

Maybe I could pretend I lost my sheet music! No, Mrs. Harmon would probably just whip out a spare copy.

Maybe I could say my hand was injured! No, Momma would just take me to the doctor. Then she'd really be mad if she found out that my hand was in perfect condition and she had a doctor bill to pay.

Maybe if I told Momma how mean Mrs. Harmon is to me, she wouldn't make me play in the recital. Maybe she'd be so upset that she'd let me quit taking piano lessons. Yes! That plan would probably work! I couldn't wait until Momma got home so I could talk to her. I could even make myself cry when I got to the part about Mrs. Harmon smacking my hand. I could throw my arms around Momma's neck and sob like they do in the movies. No, that might overdo it.

I went into the bathroom and stood in front of the mirror. I quietly practiced what I was going to tell Momma. When I got to the part about Mrs. Harmon hitting my hand, I tried to squeeze out some tears. It wasn't working. I knew just what to do! Onions! Onions always make my eyes water. I ran into the kitchen to get a few slices to rub on my hands. I wanted to be ready when Momma got home.

The minute I walked into the kitchen, Sandra started nagging me.

"Come on, Sharie," Sandra said. "You need to dry these dishes and put them away."

"You are not the boss of me, and you can't tell me what to do."

"You just wait until Momma gets home," Sandra said. "You're going to wish you had put these dishes up."

The phone rang. We both rushed to answer it, but Sandra got there first.

"It's Annette," Sandra said. "You better hurry up and get off that phone and help me with these dishes."

"Momma only said I had to help Miss Perfect," I yelled back as I ran into the living room to grab the phone, "she didn't say when."

"Hey, Annette," I said. "What's up?"

"I just called to see if you wanted to go to Joyland on Saturday."

"I'd love to go!" I said. "I'm pretty sure Momma will drop us off, now that we're old enough to ride all the rides by ourselves."

"That's right! I forgot all about that," Annette said. "Can you come and pick me up?"

"I don't think Momma will mind," I said. "I can

hardly wait until Saturday. I've always wanted to ride on the Scream-a-rama."

"Sharie, get in here right now!" Sandra shouted into the kitchen phone. "Or I'm going to tell Momma on you!" That's her favorite sentence. I'll bet she learned to say that before she learned how to say her own name.

I just kept on holding the phone and ignoring Sandra. I didn't want her to think I would hang up because she was bossing me around. Before I knew what was happening, Sandra started screaming at me. So I screamed back.

"Sharie, get in here and dry these dishes!" Sandra shouted into the phone. "I can't clean off the cabinet and mop the floor until you finish your share of the work."

"Take a chill pill, Sandra," I said stubbornly.

That made Sandra furious. She started going on and on about how much trouble I was getting myself into! I tried to ignore her, but she was shouting so loudly I could barely hear Annette.

21

"Bye, Sharie," Annette finally shouted into the phone. "I'm hanging up now."

"You don't have to hang up," I said. "She's not my momma."

"Thank goodness," said Sandra into the phone. "I'd hate to have to claim you as my child! I don't know what I did to deserve a sister like you anyway!"

Boy, that really hurt my feelings. I wasn't going to let Sandra get away with that. I was going to get even!

Chapter Five

The Argument

Sandra and I started to call each other names. Before I knew it, I heard a click on the phone. Annette had hung up. Sandra and I suddenly stopped screaming at each other. It seemed stupid to be yelling into the phone when we were in the same house.

"You're so ugly, Sandra, you have to sneak up on a glass of water," I said before I slammed the phone down in her ear.

Sandra stormed into the living room. "I'm sick and tired of you getting away with everything just because you're the youngest. And I'm tired of taking all the blame!"

"Me!" I shouted back. "You're the one who gets

away with everything! All I hear is *Sandra* this, and *Sandra* that. *Sandra's* doing so well in school. *Sandra* is so talented. I'm sick of hearing your name. Momma never says anything nice about me!"

"You're crazy!" Sandra said. "Momma lets you do whatever you want and then blames me if something goes wrong. And besides all that, you're Daddy's baby girl."

"Oh, come on, Sandra! Momma and Daddy brag on you so much it makes me want to hurl. The last time we had company, Momma showed everyone your report card. She hardly said a word about me."

"Oh, please," Sandra said. "How would you like it if you had to do everything perfectly because you're the oldest? How would you like it if everyone expected you to act like a grown-up even though you're still a kid?"

"No one *makes* you practice four hours a day or bring home straight A's. You just like making me look bad and getting me into trouble. No one is putting any pressure on you, Miss Perfect. You're just a big show-off."

Sandra looked so mad I thought she was going to hit me. She clenched her teeth, balled up her fists, and went into her room. She slammed the door so hard the walls shook.

I went into the kitchen and started to put up the dishes. I hate arguing with Sandra. If she wouldn't yell at me, I wouldn't mind helping out. But most of the time she says stuff in a real bossy tone of voice and then we start fighting. And she always tattles on me as soon as Momma steps in the door.

Momma works in a factory, so she has pretty weird hours. Her schedule depends on how busy they are. I know she's trying hard to take care of us, but I wish she had a job with regular hours. My dad is in the navy and right now he's at sea. He's been gone for almost a year. He writes to us, but it's just not the same. We all miss him a lot, and Momma gets real sad sometimes.

Momma always leaves Sandra in charge. That's what causes all the problems between us. Sandra is bossy and rude when Momma's gone and sweet as pie when she's at home. Sandra talks to me like I'm three years old and left my brain in the refrigerator!

As soon as Momma got home from work, Sandra started tattling on me. Momma didn't even have time to put her purse down.

"Momma, Sharie wouldn't help me with the dishes."

"You're a big liar, Sandra," I said. "Listen, Mom, I need to talk to you about something."

"Sharie, don't call your sister a liar," Momma said wearily. She picked up the mail that was on the hall table. Then she sat down in the old recliner in the living room.

"Mom . . ." I started again.

"Here's a letter from your daddy," Momma said happily.

"What I have to say will only take a minute," I tried again.

"Guess what!" Momma said. "Your daddy will be home sometime in the next two or three days. He's not sure what day, but he'll let us know!" She smiled at us and waved the letter in the air.

"Yeah!" I yelled. I reached for the letter so I could read it. Sandra reached for it at the same time. I tugged on it. She tugged back. The letter lost. It tore in half.

Momma stared at me. "Oh, Sharie, now look what you've done!"

"Momma, I had the letter first," I shouted angrily. "You never listen to my side."

"Don't you raise your voice to me, girl!"

I got so mad that I lost my temper again. I told Momma that I wished I had another mother and was in a different family.

Momma looked like I had slapped her. Even Sandra was speechless for once in her life. She reached over and put her arm around Momma's shoulders. I felt terrible. When would I learn to keep my big mouth shut? I wondered what was going to go wrong next.

Chapter Six

Me and My Big Mouth

Everybody got real quiet after I said I wished I had another mother. Momma had a hurt look in her eyes.

"That was a mean thing to say," Sandra said. "You ought to apologize to Momma right now."

"Why don't you mind your own business, Sandra?" I snapped.

"You two stop arguing!" Momma shouted. She looked real tired and sad. I couldn't stand to look at her. My big mouth had gotten me into trouble again. Every time I thought I was going to change my ways, something happened that made me get into even more trouble. I was angry, but not at Sandra or

Momma. I was mad at myself for saying such mean things.

I started crying. I ran into my room, flopped down on the bed, and put my pillow over my face. I didn't want anybody to see me. A little while later, I heard the door opening up real slow.

"Sharie, I want to talk to you," Momma said quietly.

She just stood by the door like she was waiting for something. I guess she thought I was going to start screaming again. I took the pillow off my face and sat up. I felt hot all over as if I was running a fever.

"Look, Sharie," Momma said. "I know what it's like to have a hot temper and say things you don't mean. I was just like you when I was your age."

I was so surprised I couldn't talk. Momma had a hot temper? She was always so patient and sweet. She hardly ever even raised her voice.

"I didn't know that," I said finally.

"I remember one time, when I was about nine or ten, I got so mad at my mother that I packed my bags and ran away from home."

"You ran away from home?"

"I sure did," Momma said. "I ran about eight blocks away before I got tired. I sat down on my suitcase and thought about everything for a long time. I realized that I was the one who was wrong. I turned around and came home. My mother pretended like I had never even left."

"You didn't get into trouble?" I said. "Grandma wasn't mad at you?"

"No," Momma said. "At first, I thought she didn't care about me. Then I realized she had her hat and coat on. I guess she was just about ready to start looking for me when I came in."

"Did you get into trouble a lot?"

"Yes," Momma said, "until I finally learned how to control my temper. I try to count to twenty before I say anything."

"I guess I should try that, too," I said.

"It helps," Momma said. "Sometimes I even wait until the next day before I bring up something that's bothering me. It gives me a chance to cool off and time to think about what I'm going to say. The bad thing about words is that once they leave your mouth, you can't take them back."

"I'm sorry I hurt your feelings, Momma, but sometimes I feel like I'm the only one who ever gets into any trouble around here. You never fuss at Sandra, and you just seem to like her the best."

Momma sighed. "I love both of you just the same, Sharie. But Sandra minds me better than you do."

"Well, you should see how bossy Sandra is when you're not around. She acts like I'm supposed to do what she says the second she tells me to."

"Well, Sharie, sometimes you're just real hardheaded. Would you think it was fair if I let Sandra be bad and made you be good?"

I'd never thought about it like that. "No, Momma," I said, "that wouldn't be fair at all. I don't mean to be hard-headed, but no one ever seems to care about how I feel about anything. I'm just tired of you and Sandra always jumping on me."

"Sharie," said Momma, "I'm the one who's tired! I work myself to death, and then I come home to nothing but a house full of complaints."

I was just getting ready to defend myself when my mother put her head in her hands and started crying. I felt horrible. Now I'd never get a chance to tell her why I didn't want to play in the recital, and she certainly wasn't going to let me go to Joyland! What was I going to do?

Chapter Seven

Momma and I Make a Deal

"Don't cry, Momma," I said.

I looked around for some tissues. All I could find was a crumpled-up napkin I had put some cookies on. I smoothed out the napkin and gave it to her. She wiped her face and blew her nose.

"You just don't know how hard it is for me. Nobody appreciates anything around here," Momma said.

There were a few cookie crumbs on her face. I gently brushed them off.

"I'm sorry, Momma," I said. "Look, I'll do better. I didn't mean to make you cry. It's just that sometimes

I feel like you don't love me at all." I picked up her hand and patted it the way I used to when I was little. "All I hear is *Sandra* this, *Sandra* that, why can't you be like *Sandra*?" I felt my throat getting tight and hot. It always feels that way when I'm real upset. I swallowed and took a deep breath. Somebody needed to stay calm around here.

"Sharie, I didn't realize I was doing that all the time," Momma said. "I don't love Sandra any more than I love you. It's just that I have to fuss at Sandra a lot less. You get mad and fly off the handle with that hot temper of yours and get sassy."

"I'm sorry, Momma."

"You know what, Sharie?"

"What?"

"I think the main problem is that you and I just don't get to talk to each other enough."

"That's true, Momma. Like tonight for instance, I was trying to talk to you, but you ignored me."

"I didn't mean to do that," Momma said sadly. "I'm so tired most of the time when I get home, I don't know if I'm coming or going. I didn't mean to start crying. I guess I just miss your daddy. I'm glad he's finally coming home."

"Me, too," I said. I gave her a big hug. "I know you're doing the best you can."

Momma smiled at me. "From now on, Sharie, please tell me if you're having any problems. I promise to listen."

"And I promise not to be so hot tempered and sassy," I said. We smiled at each other.

"Sandra," Momma called, "will you come here please?"

Sandra opened the door so quickly I just knew she had been listening. She's so nosey, she probably had her big ear stuck against the door.

"Sandra," Momma said, "I'm tired of all this fussing and fighting. From now on, I'm going to divide the housework evenly. Each of you will be responsible for your own set of chores. That way I won't have to listen to any more tattling when I come in from work. If either of you have been lazy, I can tell who's at fault right away. Does that sound fair to you?"

"Whatever you want to do is fine with me, Momma," Sandra said.

I smiled real big. No more tattling from Miss Perfect!

Momma grinned at both of us. "I'll bet the neighbors think we're crazy. All that crying and door slamming. It sounded like a soap opera in here."

We all laughed.

"Okay, enough of this craziness. Let's get ready for bed," said Momma. She kissed both of us goodnight and glanced at my hair. It was sticking up even more than usual from all the excitement.

"Sharie," Momma said, "wash your hair when you take your bath tonight. I'll get you up early in the morning and fix it before you go to school. I almost forgot about your piano recital tomorrow night. I want both of you to look real nice."

I felt the smile slip off my face. Sandra glanced at me and grinned. She looked as if she was going to say something to Momma. I glared at her and she closed her big mouth.

Boy, just when Momma and I start to get along

better, here comes trouble. I never had a chance to tell her that I had no intention of playing in that old piano recital.

Suddenly, I thought of a brilliant plan. I knew how I could get out of playing in that recital and not make Momma mad! Then I could go to Joyland and ride the roller coaster. I couldn't wait until it was morning so that I could put my escape plan into action!

Chapter Eight

Dr. Martin's Stomacheze

The sound of Momma's alarm clock woke me up. I let my eyes get used to the dark and stretched. I knew Momma would be in to wake me up real soon so she could do my hair. That made me think about my plan for getting out of playing in the recital.

I heard her getting out of bed and the *shush-shush* sound of her houseshoes coming down the hallway. I waited until she was just outside my door. As I saw the doorknob turn, I sat up in the bed and hugged my stomach. Then I started moaning and rocking back and forth. Timing was an important part of my plan.

Momma came in the room and switched on the light. "Sharie, what's the matter with you?" she asked.

"Oh, my stomach hurts," I moaned.

I rocked back and forth a little more. I didn't want to overdo it.

"Oh, brother," Momma said, "of all days. How long has it been hurting?"

"Oh, not too long, Momma," I said. Well, that was true anyway.

Momma left the room and started to rummage around in the medicine cabinet. Then she went into the kitchen. I heard her getting something out of the silverware drawer. She came back with a tablespoon and the large, economy-size bottle of Dr. Martin's Stomacheze.

Momma poured a huge spoonful of the thick, chalky-colored medicine onto the spoon. She held it out for me to swallow. Dr. Martin's Stomacheze smells and tastes like a sweaty tennis shoe. The medicine covered my tongue, slid down my throat, and landed with a thud. I could feel it swirling around inside my empty stomach like it was unclogging a sink.

"That ought to do it," said Momma as she shook the bottle. "I'm going to have to get some more of this stuff. We're almost out."

I let out another groan. This time I wasn't faking.

"Sharie, you should feel better in a little while. I'm going to get dressed and then I'll do your hair." Momma patted my hand and read the label on the bottle. "'QUICK RESULTS GUARANTEED WITH EIGHT BIG DOSES OF STOMACHEZE.' Just to be on the safe side we'll dose you with this medicine every four hours. You can skip school today and just rest. By tonight you'll feel as good as new."

Momma smiled happily. "I know you've been working hard on your piano lessons. I don't want you to have to miss your recital."

She patted my hand again and went back into her room humming a little tune.

I held my stomach. Dr. Martin's Stomacheze made me feel real queasy. All I could do was moan. I have to take that stinky, horrible medicine every four hours. And I still have to play in that dumb old recital. Boy, my escape plan failed big time. I could have cried. I had forgotten all about that stinky medicine! My plan was to play sick so that Momma would let me skip the piano recital. I should have known better!

Momma got dressed and told me to come and get my hair done. She was going to press and curl my hair so it would look nice for the recital.

Momma tried putting a perm on my hair once. It looked nice for a couple of days. Then my hair started to fall out by the handfuls. I was afraid I was going to wake up one morning and be as bald as a light bulb. For a while, I thought I was going to have to wear a wig like my Aunt Cheryl. She doesn't have very much hair to pin the wig on to. It's always slipping from one side to the other.

In a way I guess it's a lot easier if you don't have any hair. I'm sure bald people just take a wet rag and polish their heads in the morning. Then they can just let their heads air dry. Just the same, I was real happy when my hair finally stopped falling out. Momma said it was a good thing my hair is so thick, because you could hardly tell I'd lost any. I guess she was right, because no one at school asked me if I was going bald.

I decided I'd try to talk to Momma about staying home from the recital while she was doing my hair.

But how could I be too sick to play in the recital on Friday night, but well enough to ride the Scream-a-rama roller coaster at Joyland on Saturday? I knew just what to do!

Chapter Nine

Home Sick

I went into the kitchen and sat on one of the stools. Momma got her old iron pressing comb and the metal curling iron out of the drawer. She let them heat up on the stove. She unbraided my plaits one by one and combed through each of them with the pressing comb. Momma can press my hair real fast. In no time, my hair was straight and smooth.

Momma tested the curling iron on a napkin to make sure it wasn't too hot. She curled my hair into tight ringlets.

"Momma," I began. "Can I talk to you about something?"

"Sharie, honey, can we talk about it when I get

home? I'm running late and I want to give you my full attention."

"Okay, Momma," I said. That ruined part of my plan, but I figured I could talk to Momma as soon as she came home.

"Now," said Momma as she curled the last lock of hair, "you look real pretty." She glanced at the clock. "I need to get out of here. I don't want to be late for work."

I went to look at myself in the bathroom mirror. Without my glasses, I look kind of like my Momma.

"Don't try to style your hair, Sharie," Momma said. "You'll have it looking like a chicken's nest."

I put my glasses back on and turned off the bathroom light. I passed by Sandra's room. She was pretending her hairbrush was a microphone and that she was a singer.

"Quit trying to sing," I said. "Can't you hear the dogs howling outside?"

"You are *so* funny," Sandra said. "And you're going to be *so* late if you don't hurry up and get dressed. Aren't you going to school?"

"Duh, I usually don't go to school in my pajamas, Super Brain," I said crossly. My head and stomach were killing me.

Sandra grinned at me. "Well," she said, "your pajamas look better than what you usually wear to school. At least they match."

I was too sick to throw anything at her. Besides, it was true. I don't care too much about clothes. I usually pick up my clothes off the floor and put on whatever smells the best.

"What are you going to do about the recital?" Sandra asked.

"I wish you would leave me alone," I said. "Just let me worry about my own business." I held my stomach and rolled over. Some people simply have no respect for a person's privacy. I thought I was going to have to threaten her again about old Robert Nickols. For once she closed her mouth and left me alone.

Momma came into the room to check on me before she left for work.

"Well, you're not running a fever," she said as she felt my forehead. "That Stomacheze ought to have you feeling better soon. I'll call you when I get my break to see how you're doing. I want to make sure you take your medicine on time."

Momma kissed me good-bye. "Let's go, Sandra," she said.

Miss Perfect continued to stare at herself in the mirror until Momma switched off the light. Sandra would rather look at herself than watch TV.

After they were gone, I started to worry about the recital. I didn't know my music. Mrs. Harmon was sure to tell Momma about how I had acted. On top of that, my stomach was killing me. It wouldn't do any good to tell Momma my stomach still hurt. She'd probably just whip out the Stomacheze and make me swallow the whole bottle.

I finally decided there was nothing I could do but try to play the first six notes of "The Babbling Brook" and run out of the recital. Then I had a sudden thought. Maybe I could practice right now and learn the rest of the song! Maybe if I worked all afternoon, I would sound good enough so that no one would laugh at me.

I sat up quickly. The room started to spin like a

merry-go-round. I staggered into the living room to practice. The music looked blurry and I couldn't find the right keys. Well, maybe I could just play the first six notes over and over and over and no one would notice.

I went back to bed. I could almost feel that Stomacheze sloshing around in my stomach. This wasn't how I'd planned things at all. I was going to pretend to be sick to get out of the piano recital, but now I *really* felt bad. Worst of all, if I was this sick now, how was I going to go to Joyland with Annette on Saturday? Momma would probably make me stay in bed the whole weekend!

I had really messed this up big time. Unless I could think of something — and fast — I was going to have one of the worst summers of my life!

Chapter Ten

The Piano or the Stomacheze?

I must have fallen asleep because the next thing I knew, the phone was ringing and ringing in the living room. I swung my legs over the side of the bed and stood up. I still felt dizzy. I went into the living room and picked up the receiver.

"Hello," I said sleepily.

"How are you feeling, Baby?" Momma asked.

"About the same, Momma."

"Well," said Momma, "take some more Stomacheze and get plenty of rest. I'll be home early today so I won't miss the recital. Take care, now. I've got to go."

"Bye, Momma," I said.

Take some more Stomacheze? No way! I flipped on the TV. There was nothing on but talk shows and soap operas. I couldn't find anything I wanted to watch. It was the last day of school, summer was almost here, Daddy was coming home, Annette wanted me to go to Joyland, and I was too sick to be happy about anything! I turned off the television and went back to bed.

The sound of Sandra banging open my door woke me up. I yawned and glanced at the clock. It was 5:30! I'd slept almost all day. I guess that Stomacheze has knockout drops in it, too!

"Momma says you'd better get ready, Sharie," Sandra said. "We've got to leave in an hour."

I got out of bed and went into the bathroom. I felt real shaky. I didn't know if it was because I was nervous or if the Stomacheze was making me shake like that. I scooped up a handful of cold water and splashed it on my face. I still felt weird, but there was nothing I could do about it. Momma knocked on the door.

"Hurry up and put on your new dress, Sharie,"

she called. "Then I'll comb your hair. I want to get to the recital early so I can get a good seat."

I opened the door. "I don't feel so good, Momma," I said.

"Well, that Stomacheze has always worked before," she said. "It's probably time for another dose."

"Oh, that's okay," I said quickly. "I feel better than I did this morning!"

I quickly closed the door before she could say anything else. I couldn't take any more of that stuff. I'd rather play in the recital than swallow another spoonful of that thick, awful, chalky-tasting stuff.

I went into my room and put on my new dress. It was the only one they had at Daughty's Department Store in the "Large Little Ladies" Department that fit me. The dress is a real ugly green with a huge sailor collar and big white anchors all over it. It made me feel seasick.

Sandra was dressed and ready to go. She looked real nice in her new blue suit. Knowing Sandra, she'd probably be doing some real fancy moves on the keyboard. Sandra always wants everyone to think she's so cool. Momma had on her lemon yellow suit. Everyone looked slim and trim but me. I felt like a battleship. There was nothing I could do about it now.

Momma quickly combed through my hair. I had squashed most of the curls flat on one side while I was asleep. Half of my hair looked pretty and curly. The other half looked droopy and limp.

"It doesn't look too bad," Momma said. "It'll have to do for now. We need to go."

I looked at my hair. It looked terrible! I put some water on the comb and tried to get the curly side to look a little less curly. *Oops!* Too much water! My hair was soaking wet. It dripped down into my eyes. It was a soggy mess on one side and slightly curly on the other. I grabbed a towel and tried to dry my hair. It began to get frizzy and stand up all over my head. I looked like Big Bird on Sesame Street. I slicked my hair back into a ponytail. It was still sticking up in places, but there was nothing I could do.

"Sharie," Momma said, "we need to go! What's

taking you so long? Oh, my goodness! What have you done to your hair?"

"I was trying to fix it, but it just looks worse," I said.

"Well, it's too late to do anything about it now. You'll just have to wear it like that. All that work for nothing! Let's go."

I was shaking on the inside. Momma was furious about my hair. Mrs. Harmon was probably going to tell on me tonight. I had to play in the recital, and on top of all that, my head and stomach felt awful.

As soon as we walked in the door, Mrs. Harmon rushed over to us. Boy, did she look mad!

Chapter Eleven

Mrs. Harmon Talks to Momma

As soon as Mrs. Harmon got close to us, I began to bite my nails. I knew I was in big trouble.

"Mrs. Johnson," said Mrs. Harmon, "I need to talk with you about Sharie."

Uh-oh, I thought, *here it comes.* I tried to slip away, but Mrs. Harmon shot out her chubby hand and grabbed my arm.

"I haven't been getting the cooperation I need to make this recital a success," Mrs. Harmon wheezed. She glared at me and wetly adjusted her dentures. I felt so scared my knees started to knock together.

"We need someone to announce each child before they play," said Mrs. Harmon. She tugged on her wig and slipped her upper dentures around in her mouth. "I'd do it myself, but I need to keep order backstage. The other children are too shy to stand in front of everyone. I know Sandra would do a wonderful job, but she's playing our grand finale. I wanted to save her wonderful song as a surprise. As you know, your Sharie is very talkative. I thought she could play her song first and then announce each child after her."

Momma looked pleased about the idea. "I'm sure Sharie would love to help you, Mrs. Harmon," Momma said. She smiled at me.

I felt so relieved I almost smiled back. Maybe Mrs. Harmon wouldn't tell on me after all. Then I realized that Mrs. Harmon knew I wouldn't be able to refuse, not after the way I had acted yesterday. I looked at Mrs. Harmon and tried to smile.

"What do you want me to read?" I asked.

Mrs. Harmon put a piece of paper in my hands and glared at me. "All you have to do is read this just as it is written," she said, clicking her dentures to-gether.

I moved out of spit firing range and glanced at the

program. Mrs. Harmon has funny handwriting. I could barely make it out, but I was too scared to say anything.

"I'm sure Sharie will do just fine," said Momma.

Mrs. Harmon gave me a threatening look. "I'm sure she will, Mrs. Johnson," she said. "Come along, Sharie and Sandra, the program starts soon." Mrs. Harmon grabbed my arm again and marched me off to the back of the stage.

Sandra tagged along behind us but paused long enough to smile at Robert Nickols. At first I thought he came to hear Sandra play. Then I remembered that his brother, Marcus, took lessons from Mrs. Harmon, too.

There were about thirty kids backstage. Most of them were talking noisily or running around. I didn't recognize anyone but Marcus. As soon as he saw me, he pointed at my dress and whispered into another boy's ear. They both looked at me and burst out laughing.

Mrs. Harmon clapped her hands together. "Ladies and gentlemen, let me have your attention please."

The kids quieted down a little bit and looked at Mrs. Harmon.

"Our program will be starting soon. Sharie Johnson will be our mistress of ceremonies. She will play her song first, then she'll call out your name and the name of the song you'll be playing. Listen very closely. When you hear your name, walk quickly on to the stage, play your song, bow, and exit."

She began lining everyone up.

"Go on the stage and read the welcome I've written out, Sharie," Mrs. Harmon said. "Then play your song and announce the next name."

I looked at the paper again. My hands were so sweaty, some of the writing had smeared. My stomach churned queasily. Maybe if I told Mrs. Harmon I was deathly ill I could get out of this mess.

"Go on," she hissed. "Read the welcome speech and play your song." She pushed me through the curtains. I heard a few people giggle as I stumbled out onto the stage. I looked out at all those people in the audience. There seemed to be hundreds of eyes staring at me.

"Welcome," I croaked hoarsely. There was silence in the room. Sweat popped out on my forehead. My hands felt cold and clammy. My knees clanged together. I wished my dress was long enough to cover them. I swallowed, opened my mouth, and closed it again. I bet I looked like a big green fish.

I tried to read Mrs. Harmon's handwriting, but it was no use. I felt sick and hundreds of people were watching me make a fool of myself. I clenched my hands to my side. I wasn't going to let them laugh at me. I would just have to make something up. But what?

Chapter Twelve

The Mistress of Ceremonies

"Welcome," I said again, a little louder into the microphone. The room was deathly quiet. I wiped my face and stumbled on, talking even faster.

"I don't know who is more nervous here tonight, the kids or the parents."

To my surprise, everyone laughed! They weren't laughing *at* me. They thought I was being funny! I smiled, took a deep breath, and instantly felt better.

"Everybody relax and enjoy the show," I said. "No one ever went deaf from listening to a few wrong notes."

I crossed my eyes and touched my tongue to the tip of my nose.

The audience laughed loudly. Hey, this wasn't so bad after all.

Then, all of a sudden I had another great idea! I could announce everyone's name but my own! I wouldn't have to play and no one would know the difference until after the program was over! It would be too late then for Momma or Mrs. Harmon to do anything about it. Besides, it would be better for them to be mad at me than to make a fool out of myself in front of all these people.

I glanced down at Mrs. Harmon's spidery handwriting and announced the name after mine on the list. "Now I present Henry Davis. Henry will play 'The Spinning Song.' Make us dizzy, Henry," I said.

The audience laughed again. Mrs. Harmon gave me a puzzled look. Then she sent Henry out on stage. While he was playing, I made out the next name and song on the program. I thought of something funny to say. Henry finished his song, bowed, and left. The audience clapped.

I said something silly about each song to make the

audience laugh. By the time Sandra played her fancy grand finale, I was the hit of the show!

I had Mrs. Harmon and all the students come out and take a bow like they do on television. There was a big round of applause from the audience. Then Mrs. Harmon took over and made a little speech, thanking everyone under the sun, including me! She said I did a great job! The audience clapped the loudest for me! I couldn't believe it. They liked me! They really liked me! I smiled and took another bow. I finally did something right!

There was a lot of commotion after the program, so I slipped outside without anyone noticing me. I ran to the car as fast as I could and slid into the back seat. I was safe from Momma and Mrs. Harmon for a little while anyway.

Then I saw Momma and Sandra walking toward the car. Suddenly, Mrs. Harmon ran after them, and started waving Momma down like a traffic cop.

"Mrs. Johnson," I heard her say. "I'd like a word with you, please."

Sandra got in and shut the car door. I thought she

was going to tease me, but she didn't. We sat in silence for what seemed like hours.

I felt terrible. Mrs. Harmon was probably telling Momma about everything I'd done. How I had lost my temper, how I didn't read what she had written for the program, and worst of all, how I knew I was supposed to play first for the recital but had skipped my name. Momma would probably ground me until it was time for me to go to college. I wouldn't get a chance to ride the Scream-a-rama at Joyland until I was old and gray.

It seemed like no matter how hard I tried, I was always in the doghouse with Momma. Hot tears slid down my face. I wiped my eyes and sniffled quietly so Sandra wouldn't know how upset I was and make fun of me.

"Quit crying, Sharie," Sandra said.

"Leave me alone," I said. I tried to stop crying, but it seemed like the tears started sliding down my cheeks even faster. I was so tired of being in trouble all the time.

"Don't worry," Sandra said. "I'll tell Momma Mrs.

Harmon was always hitting your hands. You know Momma won't like that. Maybe she'll understand why you were so mad and hated playing the piano."

I was so shocked that Sandra was going to defend me that I quit crying. I couldn't believe my sister was actually going to do something nice for me.

"Thanks, Sandra," I said.

"Wipe your eyes and blow your nose," Sandra said as she handed me a tissue. "Here comes Momma, and she's not smiling."

Chapter Thirteen

Sharie Tells the Truth

Momma was real quiet when she got in the car. No one said a word. When we got home, I started to go directly into our room, but Momma stopped me.

"Sharie, come in my room, please. I want to talk to you."

I knew that I was in big trouble. I followed Momma into her room and closed the door. She sat down on the side of the bed.

"Why didn't you tell me you were doing so badly with the piano?"

"Oh, Momma," I said, "I did try to tell you, but you said I'd do better if I just practiced more."

"Well," said Momma. "I thought that would help.

But tonight Mrs. Harmon told me something about you that really surprised me."

I broke out in a sweat. "Momma," I said quickly, "let me tell you my side of the story first."

"No, let me finish," Momma said. "Mrs. Harmon said she thinks you ought to give up the piano. She said you have a wonderful way with words and that you should study acting or public speaking. She said that's where your real talent is."

I could hardly believe my ears! Mrs. Harmon said something nice about me. And best of all, no more piano lessons! I screamed, clapped my hands, and hugged Momma around the neck.

"Girl, you're a mess," Momma said as she untangled my arms. "Now, let me hear your side of the story."

There was no way I was going to tell Momma what I'd said to Mrs. Harmon.

"It's not important," I said.

"You were just pretending you were sick, weren't you?" Momma asked.

I nodded my head yes. Momma looked serious. She hates for us to tell a lie. "Well, I guess you will make a good actress. You sure fooled me!"

"Well, Momma," I said, "my stomach was kind of upset because I was so nervous about the recital. But I really got sick when you gave me that Stomacheze!"

We laughed until tears filled our eyes.

"I guess you've been punished enough for one day," Momma said. "Go to bed."

"Goodnight, Momma," I said. "I wouldn't trade you for any momma in the whole wide world."

"Goodnight, crazy girl," Momma said, smiling. "I wouldn't trade you either."

"Momma," I said. "Will you please, please, take me and Annette to Joyland tomorrow? We can ride all the rides by ourselves now. And I promise I'll do all my chores first."

"If you finish your chores, I'll take you," Momma said.

I jumped off the bed, danced to the door, and flung it open. Sandra almost fell into the room. She'd been listening so hard I guess she forgot to move away from the door when she heard me coming. I grabbed her arm to keep her from falling down.

"No more piano lessons!" I said, smiling happily. "Plus, I get to go to Joyland with Annette tomorrow!"

I hugged Sandra and gave her one of my extra special, double drippy, sloppy wet kisses on the cheek.

"Yuck," said Sandra as she wiped her face, but she was smiling.

"Now maybe the piano will stay in tune since you won't be banging on it anymore."

We all laughed.

"Go to bed now," Momma said. "I don't know exactly what time your daddy's coming home tomorrow night, but I want everything to be ready for him when he gets here."

"I'm going to music camp in the morning, but I'll be back pretty early," Sandra said. "I can't wait to see Dad."

"I'm going to make him an extra-special dinner," Momma said. "Steak, mashed potatoes, green beans, and apple pie."

"Apple pie!" I said. "I love apple pie."

"I thought you were sick," Sandra teased.

"I was," I said. "But the minute Momma said I didn't have to play the piano anymore and that I could go to Joyland, I was cured."

I spun Sandra around and around until we were both dizzy. We collapsed on the floor. The room was tilting from side to side.

"Okay, enough you two!" Momma said. "Go to bed!"

I danced down the hallway. What a day! School was finally out! No more piano lessons! I could go with Annette to Joyland! And best of all, Daddy was coming home! Now everything was just great except for one small problem. Where was I going to get the money to spend at Joyland?

Chapter Fourteen

Money Trouble

I opened my eyes and stretched. Ah, the first day of summer vacation. This was going to be wonderful!

I could hear Momma out in the hallway sorting out the dirty laundry. I could tell exactly what she was doing even though I couldn't see her. The metal hangers she always uses to hang up the clothes jingled like new money.

Money! My eyes popped wide open. I needed to earn some money fast if I was going to Joyland. All I had to my name was three dollars.

I could hear Momma coming down the hall. I pretended like I was still asleep.

"Sharie," said Momma, "hurry and get up! Take

those sheets off your bed. I put your list of chores on the refrigerator. I'm going to start the wash."

"Momma, if I get through with all my chores, will you give me some extra money? I want to ride all the rides at Joyland."

"We'll see," Momma said. "The faster you work, the more money you earn."

I jumped out of bed and stripped the sheets off the mattress. Then I looked around on the floor for my blue jeans. I couldn't find a clean blouse, so I borrowed one of Sandra's shirts. She had already left to go to music camp. I knew she would be mad if she saw me wearing her shirt, but I didn't care. The last time I wore one of her shirts she said it was a smelly, dirty mess and it was hard to get all the stains out of it. I had accidentally spilled ketchup and mustard on it at lunch. I didn't think she'd notice, but she did. When I told her they had a new invention that took care of dirty clothes, called a washing machine, she threw the shirt in my face. It smelled so bad I couldn't breathe, but I didn't tell her that.

I found my hightops under the bed. The green

socks I wore yesterday were still stuffed inside of them, so I didn't have to look for a clean pair. I couldn't find my comb, so I just ran my fingers through my hair and twisted it into a ponytail. At last I was ready.

I rushed through my housework as fast as I could. I made up my bed and cleaned my room. Some things I stuffed into my dresser drawers. Other junk I just stuffed under the bed. I decided to fool with it all later. I dusted off my dresser and bookcase with the inside of my shirt. The room looked pretty good, so I moved on to the next chore on Momma's list.

It was my turn to vacuum and clean the bathroom. I hate cleaning the bathroom. I'd almost rather wash dishes than clean the bathroom, and I really hate washing dishes. I whipped the vacuum cleaner around the carpets as fast as I could. Then I scrubbed the bathroom tile and cleaned the sink and the toilet bowl. Our bathroom is so old that all the plumbing fixtures look like something out of a horror movie. Momma tried to make it look pretty with new paint and a matching rug and shower set. Even with all the ruffles, the tub and sink just sort of squat there like big, white mushrooms after a hard rain.

"All done, Momma!" I yelled.

Momma looked around the living room, in my bedroom, and in the bathroom. I held my breath. I hoped she didn't look under the bed or open my dresser drawers. If she did, I was sunk. She didn't.

"Okay," Momma said. "Here's five dollars."

"I'm rich, I'm rich!" I yelled.

"You wish," Momma said. "Let's go pick up Annette."

I tucked the money into the jean pocket that had three dollars in it. Then I ran out to the car. Annette was waiting for us on her front porch when we drove up.

"Hello, Mrs. Johnson," Annette said politely. "Thank you for picking me up."

"You're welcome, sweetie," Momma said.

Annette is so ladylike and girly-girly. Momma thinks that I should act more like her. No way!

"Did you know that the Scream-a-rama is the tallest, fastest wooden roller coaster in the whole world?" I said to Annette as she slid next to me in the back seat.

"I don't know if I want to ride the Scream-a-rama."

I looked at Annette as if she had lost her mind. There was no way I was going to miss out on riding the Scream-a-rama, but I didn't want to hurt her feelings. I'd just have to find a way to trick Annette into getting on the Scream-a-rama. But how?

Chapter Fifteen

Joyland

"Sharie, I don't want you riding that roller coaster by yourself," Momma said. "If Annette doesn't want to ride, then you stay off of it. Okay?"

"Oh, Momma," I said, "I've been looking forward to riding the Scream-a-rama for days."

"I don't care," Momma said. "I want you two to stay together."

"Don't worry, Mrs. Johnson," Annette said. "Whatever we do, I promise we'll do it together."

"Good," Momma said. "It'll be safer if you stick together."

"We'll be careful," I said. If Annette didn't want to

ride the Scream-a-rama, she was going to ruin all my fun!

"Look," I whispered, "if you promise to ride the Scream-a-rama with me, you can pick everything else we do tonight okay?"

"I'll think about it," Annette whispered back.

"What are you two whispering about?" Momma asked.

"I wanted to make sure Annette brought her money," I said. I poked Annette in the ribs with my elbow.

"Momma gave me five dollars," Annette said quickly. "I took four more from my penny bank."

"Good," I said, pulling my money out of my jeans. "I've got eight bucks."

I grabbed the money from Annette and threw it in the air like they do on the cartoons. "We're rich! We're rich!"

Dollar bills filled the air and floated gently to the floor. Annette and I started to giggle.

"If you don't want that money, I'll take it," Momma said, glaring at us in the rearview mirror.

"Oh no, we want it," I said. I picked up the money as fast as I could. I wadded the eight ones into my jeans. Then I handed the rest of the money to Annette. Momma is real funny about money. I guess it's because she has to work so hard to earn it.

We could see the huge lights that spelled out Joyland all the way down the block. We were out of the car almost before Momma could stop.

"Hey," she yelled as we ran off. "You two better be at the front gate at 9:15!"

"We will!" I yelled back. We waved good-bye and raced to the park entrance. I craned my neck back and looked up as the roller coaster rumbled overhead.

"That's where we're going first," I said. I could hear the riders screaming as the roller coaster roared by.

I felt really grown up. This was the first time that Momma let me go to Joyland without staying or sending Sandra with me. I'd always wanted to ride on a roller coaster, but Momma would never let me.

"Come on, Annette," I yelled as I squeezed into the Scream-a-rama ticket line.

"I don't know, Sharie," said Annette, peering upward as the riders swooped by. "I'm kind of scared of that thing. Besides, you said I could pick everything else we do tonight. I don't want to ride the Scream-a-rama right now."

"Oh, Annette," I said. "Don't be such a big old baby. Look at those people on the Scream-a-rama. I bet they're laughing and having a wonderful time. We're missing out."

Of course, I couldn't hear anyone laughing, but I did hear a whole lot of screaming. The ride finally rumbled to a stop. The passengers started to get out of the cars.

"Boy," I said, "you sure have to wear a lot of safety belts."

The ride attendant was helping a man whose legs looked like they had turned to rubber. The attendant held the man's arm as he wobbled down the ramp.

"I'm sure you'll be fine after you sit down for a while," said the attendant.

Annette and I exchanged glances. Her face looked as pale as moonlight.

"Oh, don't worry about him," I said confidently. "He looked kind of old. Maybe he has a weak heart or something."

"There's no way I'm getting on that thing!" Annette said.

It was almost my turn to buy a ticket. I really wanted to ride the Scream-a-rama. I promised Momma we would stay together, and now Annette was leaving. If I didn't stay with her all night, I'd get into trouble. I was so mad at Annette I was almost crying. What was I going to do?

Chapter Sixteen

Best Friends to the End?

"Wait a minute, Annette," I shouted after her. "Aren't you going to ride with me?"

"No way!"

"Oh, Annette!" I said. "Come on or we'll lose our turn!" Annette stayed where she was. The line started to move.

I thought about riding by myself. I knew it wouldn't be any fun, and if Annette told Momma I rode on alone, I'd be in trouble. Oh, brother! I ran down the ramp after Annette.

"What's the deal?" I asked, grabbing her arm. "All you've been talking about for the last two days is the Scream-a-rama!"

"I don't want to ride it right now, Sharie," Annette said. "Why don't we drive the bumper cars, and do all the other rides first? We'll save the Scream-a-rama for last."

"Look, Annette," I said. I was beginning to get mad. "I really, really want to ride the Scream-a-rama. Why can't you be a friend and get a ticket with me?"

"Well, you said I could decide what we're going to do tonight, and I've decided I don't want to ride that stupid ride first," Annette said.

"You are such a big baby."

"No, I'm not."

"You're too scared to ride anything but the baby rides."

"Look, Sharie," Annette said. "I didn't even have to invite you to come with me tonight. I could have asked somebody else."

"Well, maybe you should have," I said.

"Oh, so it's like that, huh?" Annette said. "First you say one thing, then you get mad and change your mind."

"I just want to ride the Scream-a-rama! We can

ride any other ride you choose. But I want to ride the Scream-a-rama! Is that too much to ask?"

People swirled around us, rushing from one ride to another. I was so mad I was breathing like I'd just run a race. I closed my eyes and took a deep breath. Then I counted to twenty like Momma told me to do. Annette and I stared at each other for a minute. Annette's face was beet red.

I started to giggle. "You look like a tomato."

"And you were moving your lips while you were counting. I thought maybe you wanted to play hide-and-seek!"

We laughed so hard we had to sit down on a bench.

"We're wasting time," Annette said. "Let's go ride other rides first and save the Scream-a-rama for last. That will make it more fun."

I felt like Annette was trying to trick me. I bet she was going to try to talk me out of getting on the Scream-a-rama at the last minute. But after all, she is my best friend, and I promised to let her pick everything else we did.

"Okay," I said finally. "But only if you'll promise me that we'll stop and ride the Scream-a-rama when 8:30 comes. I want to be sure we have time to ride it before Momma comes to pick us up."

"I promise," Annette said. "Now let's ride the bumper cars."

We ran off to the bumper cars. I almost tripped over my own feet when I saw who was standing in line. Robert Nickols had just finished paying for a ticket for himself and his brother Marcus.

"Hi, Sharie," Robert said. "Where's Sandra?"

"She started music camp today," I said. I was so surprised to see him that I could barely talk.

"You and Sandra look so much alike!" he said. "I did a double-take when I saw you in her shirt. If Sandra wore glasses, you two could be twins."

Sandra and I — twins? I stood there with my mouth open. Annette nudged me and I closed it. Marcus snickered.

"Tell Sandra I said hi," Robert said as he moved toward the bumper cars.

"Oh, I will," I said. I grabbed Annette's hand. We

both started to giggle uncontrollably. Twins! Miss Perfect and a troll like me! Annette dragged me up to the ticket booth. I couldn't wait to tell Sandra what Robert said. She'd lose her lunch.

We paid for our bumper car tickets and squeezed into a bright red car. We had a great time chasing after Marcus and Robert. I was sorry when the ride was over. Annette and I ran from one ride to another. We had fun swirling around in the spinning teacups, swinging on the Ferris wheel, and riding the carousel.

Suddenly, I looked at my watch. It was 9:00! Momma was coming in fifteen minutes! Would we still have time to ride the Scream-a-rama?

Chapter Seventeen

The Ride of a Lifetime

"Hey, Annette," I said, stopping her before she could get our tickets for the stagecoach ride. "It's 9:00! We'll need to hurry if we're going to ride the Scream-a-rama before Momma comes to get us."

"Oh, Sharie," Annette said, twisting a thick lock of black hair around her fingers. "I don't know."

"Oh, come on, Annette," I said. "You promised."

"Oh, okay," Annette said. "But I'm never going to ride it again! I don't care how much you beg me. I'm only riding it one time and that's it."

"Okay," I said. "It's a deal."

We bought our tickets and got in the Scream-a-rama line. The cars were already starting to fill up.

The attendant took our tickets and strapped us in. Then he put a metal bar across our laps.

"At least we don't have to worry about falling out," I said.

"Yeah," Annette said. "Look how far we are off the ground."

I looked down. Everything seemed small and far away.

"Look how high up this thing goes," Annette said.

It sure was a long way up. I was starting to feel a little nervous, but I didn't say anything to Annette.

The cars made *click, click, click* sounds and then jerked suddenly. Annette and I were thrown back against the seat. The cars roared off down the track.

"Whoa!" I screamed. The wind was rushing past me so fast I felt like my eyeballs had been pushed back into my head. *Whoomp!* The cars dropped down a steep incline. My stomach felt like it had sunk down to my knees. I started to scream. Annette was smiling.

"This is great!" she yelled as the wind whipped through her hair. "Boy, am I glad you talked me into this." She pushed her bangs out of her eyes and smiled at me.

I was so shocked I stopped screaming. This was *great?* This was *horrible!* Here we were — about to die — and Annette was smiling.

I started to say something to her, but then the cars careened around another curve. My neck snapped back and forth like a rubber band. I clutched her arm in a death grip.

"Here we go to the top!" Annette shouted. She giggled happily.

The cars slowed down and began a jerky climb to the top of the hill. I looked over the edge of the car. Big mistake. The ground looked like it was a million miles away. I started screaming again.

My heart bumped around in my chest like a pinball machine.

"Whee!" screamed Annette. She took her hands off the guard bar and raised them into the air. I grabbed her arm and glared at her. She was trying to kill us!

"Oh, Sharie," Annette said. "You're such a big baby."

"Be quiet, Annette," I said. Up ahead I saw my worst nightmare coming true. We were going to go around a double loop before the ride came to an end.

"Whoopee!" Annette screamed. "Double loop-de-loop."

The cars gathered speed and whipped around the first loop. We were hanging upside down! I was too scared to even scream. I closed my eyes so tightly I saw stars. All of a sudden, we hurtled down to the bottom of the world. We were going so fast I thought my brain would come out of my ears. We whipped around the second loop. I was clutching the guard bar so tightly I couldn't unpry my fingers to hold my brain in! I felt another *whoomp,* and then the cars jerked to a stop.

"Sharie, come on. The ride's over." Annette had already unfastened our seat belts.

I pried my eyes open. Then I tried to get out of the car, but my legs refused to move. I checked to see if they were in their usual place. There they were, right under my knees. I had no brain left to command them to move. I'd lost it somewhere on the last loop-de-loop.

"Guess what, Sharie?" Annette said happily. "We have just enough time to ride the Scream-a-rama again!"

I was so scared that I felt like crying. There was no way I could get on the Scream-a-rama again. What if Annette told everyone we know that I am a big baby? What if she got mad at me and didn't want to be friends anymore?

Chapter Eighteen

Surprise!

Annette and the attendant lifted the steel bar. The attendant had to pull me out of the roller-coaster car. I was so dizzy I almost fell. Annette grabbed my arm and slowly walked with me as I wobbled down the steep ramp.

"I'm sure you'll be fine after you sit down for a while," said the attendant.

I tried to pretend I was okay, but I had never been so frightened in my whole life. I felt dizzy, and I couldn't keep my legs from shaking.

"Don't walk so fast, Annette," I said. She slowed down a little but started talking a mile a minute.

"Sharie, wasn't that great?" Annette said. "I loved

that double loop-de-loop! I thought I was going to come unglued when we whipped around that last curve! That was the best ride I've ever been on! Didn't you just love it?"

I looked at Annette like she had lost her mind. I snatched my arm away from her and wobbled the rest of the way down the ramp by myself. I flopped down on the bench and put my head on my knees. The whole world seemed to be spinning around and around. Annette poked me in the ribs.

"Come on, Sharie! We can ride the Scream-a-rama one more time before your momma comes to pick us up."

It took all of my strength to lift up my head and look Annette in the eye.

"I'm not going anywhere," I said.

"What?"

"I'm never, ever getting on that roller coaster again!"

"But I want to ride it one more time!" Annette said.

"Well, you'll have to go by yourself," I said quietly.

"I'd rather be grounded for the whole summer than get on that thing again. I've never been so scared in all my life."

"You were scared?" Annette said. "All you could talk about was riding the Scream-a-rama!"

"So what?" I said. "I don't care if you tell everyone we know that I'm a baby. I'm not going back on that roller coaster again — and that's it."

I got up and tried to walk to the exit gate. Everything seemed to pitch and roll, and then the world went black.

"Sharie," said a man's voice from far away. "Sharie, baby, are you all right?"

A pair of strong arms picked me up. I tried to focus my eyes, but my face was buried against a man's chest.

"Put her in the car, Howard," I heard Momma say. "She probably went out without eating and got light-headed."

The cool leather of the seat felt good against my back.

Howard? That's my daddy's name. I tried to focus

my eyes again. Annette was peering down at me. She looked scared.

"I'm okay," I said. I struggled to sit up. She pulled me up and wiped my face with her hand. Then I saw him.

"Daddy!" I screamed. I grabbed him around the neck. "I thought I was dreaming."

"No, baby, you're not dreaming," Daddy said, smiling. "But you just about scared us to death. We drove up and you were laid out on the pavement like you were dead. You really scared us."

I started to laugh and cry at the same time.

"Oh, Daddy," I said. "I'm so glad you're home. It seemed like you'd been gone forever!" We hugged each other again.

"How are you feeling?" Momma asked. "I've told you about riding those crazy rides without eating anything."

"I feel okay now, Momma," I said. I couldn't stop smiling at Daddy. I kissed him on the cheek.

"Come on, now," Momma said. "We can celebrate later. I promised to get Annette home on time."

Daddy started up the car and we headed down the road to Annette's house. We all laughed and talked at the same time.

We were a good ways from Joyland, but I could still hear faint screams floating down from the Scream-a-rama. Annette and I turned around and looked at the Joyland sign through the back window. We could see the red neon lights from the highest point of the Scream-a-rama.

"Now I know why they call it a roller coaster," I whispered. We giggled all the way home.

Dear Reader:

What Did I Do to Deserve a Sister Like You? is based on my child-hood. Like Sharie, I had wild hair, an itchy eczema rash that showed up every summer, thick glasses, a hot temper, a difficult time with piano lessons, and a beautiful older sister named Sandra.

Parts of the book are based on my actual experiences. I really did skip my name during a piano recital so I didn't have to play, and I'm still terrified of roller coasters to this day. Parts of the book are fictional and were created to tell my story.

Today, I still have wild hair and a beautiful, exceptionally tal-ented older sister named Sandra, but I've learned how to control my hot temper, the eczema is gone, and I wear contact lenses. Like Sharie, I have no musical ability, but I discovered that I love mak-ing speeches and performing. I also enjoy writing and reading what I've written in front of an audience.

More important, I've developed a friendship that I treasure with my sisters, Sandra and Marcy. While I don't write about my brother, Howard, in this series, he is also one of my dearest friends. We still tease and argue with each other, but we love each other dearly.

While I was growing up, I didn't realize the importance of my sisters and brother. Your siblings are your oldest friends. They share your genes and your history, your joys and your sorrows. They are the people who know you best; they are the ones you can always turn to; they are your family. I had to grow up to realize the importance of family.

My mother's favorite saying is: "Charity begins at home." I didn't really understand what that saying meant when I was young. Charity is another way of saying love, kindness, helping those in need, and being lenient in judging others. Now I know charity is the quality that holds families, friendships, and people together as one.

While you may not get along with your brothers and sisters now, give it time and lots of charity. Like Sharie, and like me, you'll realize that your sisters, brothers, mother, and father — your fam-ily and your friends — are precious jewels in the treasure chest of life. Show them lots of love and charity.

Love,
Angela Shelf Medearis

About the Author

Angela Shelf Medearis is an award-winning author of more than seventy books, including *Picking Peas for a Penny, Dancing with the Indians, The Ghost of Sifty-Sifty Sam, The 100th Day of School, Poppa's New Pants, The Singing Man, Annie's Gifts, Too Much Talk, The Zebra-Riding Cowboy, Rum-a-Tum-Tum, The Seven Spools of Thread,* and *Daisy and the Doll.* She also writes nonfiction books with her husband, Michael.

Angela, who lives in Austin, Texas, has been called "one of the most influential writers of children's literature in Texas" by *Texas Monthly* magazine, and rightly so. Her desire to write books for children is the result of working with second graders with reading difficulties. She went on to become the founder of *Book Boosters, Inc.,* a nonprofit organization dedicated to tutoring elementary school children who need a "boost" in their self-esteem and help with their reading.

Angela accompanied First Lady Laura Bush during a school visit in Washington, D.C., and appeared on C-Span's *Booknotes* program to do a presentation on her work.